BULLIES AT SCHOOL

Siobhan looked quickly at what had attracted her eye. On the first shelf, dusty and still, lay a coiled snake. Its black, jewelled eye, unlidded, unblinking, held hers.

As soon as Siobhan discovers the Celtic serpent brooch, her life at school starts to change. Up until then, Siobhan had been desperately unhappy, continually teased and tormented by her class-mates. But the brooch, just like the Celtic myth, gives her a strange new power to defeat her enemies . . .

Theresa Breslin is the author of *Simon's Challenge*, dramatised on BBC television, *Kezzie* and *New School Blues*. She is a popular children's author who has won the Kathleen Fidler Award and has been nominated for the Carnegie Medal and shortlisted for the Childrens Book Award.

This one is for Frances

BULLIES AT SCHOOL

Theresa Breslin

Illustrated by Scoular Anderson

CANONGATE • KELPIES

First published 1993 by Blackie
First published in Kelpies, an imprint
of Canongate Books Ltd, in 1994
This impression 1999

British Library Cataloguing-in-Publication Data
A catalogue record for this book is available
on request from the British Library.

ISBN 0 86241 494 6

Typeset by Hewer Text Composition Services, Edinburgh
Printed and bound in Denmark by Nørhaven A/S

CANONGATE BOOKS LTD,
14 HIGH STREET, EDINBURGH EH1 1TE

1

'SPECKY-WECKY FOUR-EYES! WECKY-SPECKY FOUR-EYES!'

Siobhan Cunningham hitched her school rucksack further up her back and started to walk more slowly along the road. She could now see the group at the school gate who were doing all the shouting, Karen Williams and her friends, Lyn, Rosie, Benny and Peter. They usually hung about there every morning, waiting for someone to pick on, and the someone was usually her. How things had changed! Once Rosie had been Siobhan's friend and they had always walked to school together in the mornings. Now Rosie was one of Karen's gang and Siobhan was left on her own.

Perhaps this morning she would miss her turn. They seemed to be busy with Harry

Morgan today. Siobhan really liked Harry. He sat alongside Siobhan in Miss Wainwright's class. He had a friendly smile, bright and shiny, like his glasses, and he would lend her his sharpener when she broke her pencil – which happened a dozen times a day.

'You've not broken your pencil, *again*?' Miss Wainwright would tut in annoyance as she passed their desk. 'Really, Siobhan, you must try a little harder.'

It was because she was trying so hard that

her pencil broke. She couldn't explain this to Miss Wainwright, though. Siobhan would grip it very hard between her fingers and press it on to the clean new page of her jotter. She loved doing the sentences which Miss Wainwright asked them to make up, using the words on the blackboard. Six words – six sentences. Miss Wainwright always chose interesting words, long curly ones and short snappy ones, easy ones and hard ones. Siobhan loved them all. She loved making up the

sentences. Once she had managed one whole sentence with all six words in. Miss Wainwright had been very pleased with her that day. She had read her sentence out to the whole class.

Harry had whispered 'smarty-pants' to her, but in a nice sort of a teasing tone of voice. Not the nasty way that Karen and her friends called names at people.

Only sometimes . . . when she was trying hard and spelling out a difficult word, just mouthing out the sounds, one by one under her breath, then she would be concentrating so hard on getting it right that she would lean too heavily, and the pencil point would suddenly break, leaving a squishy black smear on the bright white page. Miss Wainwright, who happened to be standing beside her desk one day, sighed and said, 'Siobhan, you really are *so* clumsy at times.'

Now, whenever Karen and her friends saw Siobhan, they screeched, 'Clumsy! Clumsy! Clumsy Cunningham!'

Siobhan was almost at the school gate. Harry had gone and they were still there. She was going to be by herself as she walked past them. Why did they always seem to pick on her? A few weeks ago she had tried to avoid them by waiting further down the road until she heard the bell ring. But Miss Wainwright had met Siobhan's mother in the supermarket and asked why she was late every day. Was there anything wrong? Her mum had asked Siobhan the same question. Siobhan had shaken her head. She was ashamed to say. Her mum had enough worries, being on her own and trying to make ends meet.

'Well, I've enough worries,' her mum had said, 'being on my own and trying to make ends meet. Don't you give me any more by getting into trouble at school. You'll need to try harder, Siobhan.'

Now Siobhan couldn't be late without having a note.

She risked a quick glance. They were whispering together. They had seen her!

Siobhan dropped her head down, swinging her shoulder-length black hair over her face. She hunched her rucksack even further up her back. She could feel the horrible sick stomach feeling starting, and the great flushing redness coming into her face. Her hands were all sweaty. Any second now and her legs were going to start to shake.

It was because she had her head down that Siobhan did not see exactly what they were up to. She was staring at her feet as she tried to be brave and walk through the gate quickly. Great big feet, she thought, as she watched them thudding along below. Clumsy, like the rest of her. Clomp, clomp, they went on the pavement, like a big horse.

'Oww!' she yelped as her face banged into the gate. She looked up quickly then all right. Just in time to see them running away, shrieking with laughter.

They had closed the gate over. She pushed at it desperately as she heard the bell ringing. It was quite a large gate, made of iron railings, and she had difficulty getting it open. At last it swung back. The bell had stopped ringing. She was going to be late! Miss Wainwright would speak to her mother again.

Siobhan raced towards the school entrance, her rucksack banging on her back. She ran through the door and then stopped for a moment in the corridor. She could feel a wet trickle on her face. She put her hand up to wipe it away and gazed in horror at her fingers. They were covered in blood!

She suddenly felt quite dizzy. Hot and faint. She would have to sit down.

'Siobhan, are you all right?' asked a sweet sugary voice.

Siobhan turned and saw Karen Williams. She knew it was her because Karen always pronounced Siobhan's name wrongly. She would say 'See-bonn', instead of 'Sha-vorn'. She was coming out of the school office with the class register in her hand.

'YOU,' shouted Siobhan. 'You stay away from me . . . you . . . you . . . bitch!'

And then as Karen came towards her Siobhan pushed her away from her with all her strength. Karen went sprawling back, straight into the arms of the Headteacher, who was coming out of the office.

When Siobhan thought about it later, she realized that Karen must have known that the Head was right behind her. That was why she had asked if Siobhan was all right in her 'butter-wouldn't-melt-in-my-mouth' voice.

'What is going on here?' the Head demanded in a loud angry voice. 'Siobhan, why did you push Karen like that?'

Siobhan hung her head down and did not reply. A large spot of blood dripped on to the floor of the corridor.

'Oh,' said the Head as she noticed it. She took a handkerchief from her pocket. 'Do you suffer from nosebleeds, Siobhan?'

Siobhan's eyes slid sideways to Karen.

'Yes,' she mumbled into the hanky. Siobhan didn't have nosebleeds, but if she said that she did, it would stop the Head asking any more questions.

The Head was furious with her. She escorted both Karen and Siobhan along the corridor. She spoke briefly to Miss Wainwright at the classroom door, Miss Wainwright gave Karen a curious look as she meekly took her seat.

Then the Head marched Siobhan to the first-

13

aid room. After Siobhan's nosebleed had stopped the Head took Siobhan to her own room and gave her a long lecture on bad temper, and being pleasant to others, and how violence would not be tolerated in her school under ANY circumstances.

Siobhan stood quietly, saying nothing. She still felt a bit sick, and anyway she thought it best not to say anything. It could only make things worse.

'And finally,' the Head said, 'I want you to give this letter to your mother. Your behaviour recently has given cause for concern. Coming in late the last few weeks, and now this.'

Siobhan stared at her. What was she saying? What letter?

The Head had been writing as she spoke. She now folded the letter over and placed it carefully in a long brown envelope. She wrote Siobhan's mother's name on the outside, stamped it firmly with the school stamp and handed it to Siobhan.

'I have explained things in this letter to your mother. You give her this when you go home tonight, and tell her I expect to hear from her in the next few days.'

3

Siobhan pushed the letter as far to the bottom of her rucksack as it would go. Right down underneath her sandwich box, beside her library book. As she walked through the office the school secretary stopped typing for a second and gave her a sympathetic look.

Siobhan hung her anorak up in the cloakroom area and went to the toilet. She looked around her. She didn't like this part of the school. It was always cold, the floors were slippery and it was a bit smelly. She shivered. Some days she spent the whole of her break in here just to avoid Karen's bossy gang. Now she took as long as she could, moving very slowly, trying to use up as much time as possible.

When she pushed open the door of her classroom everyone looked up at her, rows of staring eyes. Siobhan noticed Rosie lean over and whisper to Karen. They both tittered, and Siobhan felt a real tight pain in her chest. She and Rosie had shared so many secrets in the past, and now Rosie was laughing at her with someone else.

'Be quiet!' said Miss Wainwright crossly. 'Please take your seat, Siobhan. It's the monthly Maths class test this morning. I have left a paper on your desk.' She rapped on her own desk for attention. 'I want all of you finished by break-time.'

The Maths test! Siobhan had completely forgotten about it. Couldn't be worse, she thought. She wasn't very good at Maths at the best of times. She scraped her chair back and sat down. She took out her pencil case and stared at the paper. She couldn't do any of these problems.

The big clock on the classroom wall ticked loudly. Only a few more minutes to break, and she hadn't written anything. A big tear rolled off the end of Siobhan's nose and plopped on to her paper. Her cheeks burned hotly and she swung her hair across her face. She dabbed at the paper to dry it and the ink ran, making a

black smudge of Miss Wainwright's neat fig-
ures. Siobhan sat hopeless and miserable in her
seat.

She heard Harry beside her, shuffling his
papers noisily around on his desk. Siobhan
glanced over. He had left his answer sheet
turned towards her. He looked at her and
smiled at her from behind his glasses. He was
trying to help her!

He knew what it felt like to be picked on,
thought Siobhan. That's why he's letting me see

his work. Harry had become friends with her since last term, when they had been doing a project together. He was always happy, he just laughed when people called him names and didn't seem to mind as much as she did. He kept her cheered up. Siobhan knew she shouldn't copy. It was wrong and she never would have normally. But . . . if she took two or three answers, just this once, then at least she would have something written on her paper. Miss Wainwright would be annoyed with her if she

handed in a blank sheet. She couldn't bear another row this morning.

The bell rang and everyone got up and handed in their papers at Miss Wainwright's desk. Then they all pushed and shoved their way noisily out of the classroom.

'You may sit down and have a few more minutes, Siobhan,' said Miss Wainwright, 'to make up for lost time.' She sat at her desk correcting the papers.

Siobhan was glad to wait behind. She did not want to go out into the playground or hang around the cloakroom today. She didn't want to see or talk to anyone at all. At lunch-time she would go to the library and see if Mrs Allan, the librarian, wanted any help. Siobhan liked being in the library. It was quiet and friendly, and she was a good tidier. Mrs Allan always said so. She could eat her sandwiches there in peace.

Miss Wainwright came and stood behind Siobhan.

'Nearly time,' she said. Then she added, more gently, 'Is there anything you would like to talk to me about, Siobhan?'

Siobhan shook her head. Everyone knew

what happened if you told tales. Nobody liked sneaks.

Miss Wainwright took her paper. She glanced at it and then tutted angrily.

'Really, Siobhan, I did not expect this from *you*.' She went to the front of the classroom and picked up Harry's paper. 'If you are going to copy, dear, then try and copy from someone other than Harry. He is not very good at Maths. See?' She waved the two papers in front of Siobhan. 'You and he have exactly the same mistakes.' She sighed. 'I never thought of you as a cheat.'

Siobhan's heart was racing, and her mouth and throat were completely dry. Even if she had wanted to say something she couldn't have.

Miss Wainwright sat down at her desk and surveyed Siobhan. 'Your conduct in school gets worse and worse. I understand that the Head is sending for your mother. Well, this will be yet another subject for discussion.'

'Come on, pet, hurry up, it's nearly five thirty.'
Siobhan's mum was opening the front door as
she spoke.

Siobhan put her anorak on and came out
from her bedroom at the back of their flat.

'Don't you want to come tonight? You can
always stay next door for an hour or two,' said
her mum.

Siobhan shrugged.

'Don't mind,' she said with a sigh.

Her mum felt her forehead.

'Are you poorly? You've hardly said two
words since you came in from school. I'll get
Mrs Rogers from across the road to sit in with
you if you want to go to bed.'

'I'm coming, Mum,' said Siobhan.

Since her dad had upped and left a few years
ago her mum cleaned various offices and shops

at odd times to earn some 'extras', as she called it. Five thirty was the hairdresser's in the main street, and Siobhan had always loved going there with her mum. They usually arrived just as the staff were closing up. Mr Russell, the owner, would always come and say hello. He said she was his favourite customer and made a fuss of her and called her 'Modom', and the assistants sometimes had sweets for her.

They took the short-cut between the blocks of flats and walked towards the shops. Behind them the hills beyond the town were beginning to turn a peaty brown colour in the fading light. Siobhan liked to go out walking, or ride her bike there at the weekend. Because they lived so close to the edge of town she could be right in the country within a few minutes. It would soon be berry-picking time, and she and her mum would take a plastic pail and spend a whole Sunday gathering brambles from the hedges.

When they arrived at the hairdresser's Mr Russell sat Siobhan in one of the big black leather chairs. He swivelled her round two or three times.

'May I trim your moustache, sir?' he asked

seriously. 'Or perhaps a new wig to try?' He sat a blonde curly wig on top of Siobhan's black hair.

She giggled.

'No, I don't think so,' she drawled in a very posh voice. 'I'll just have my manicure as usual.'

Mr Russell snapped his fingers at an imaginary assistant.

'Attend to Modom. At once,' he ordered.

He put on his coat and spoke to Siobhan's mum.

'Your envelope's at the reception counter,' he said, 'just beside that new wig stand.' He took the blonde wig from Siobhan's head and returned it to the window display, then he went out of the shop.

Siobhan's mum gathered up all the towels and carried them through to the utility room to put in the washing-machine. Siobhan took the big soft brush and began to sweep up the hair from the floor. She liked doing this job. As she brushed it all into a big pile in the centre of the floor she would think of all the people who had been in the shop today. Sometimes she made up stories in her head about them.

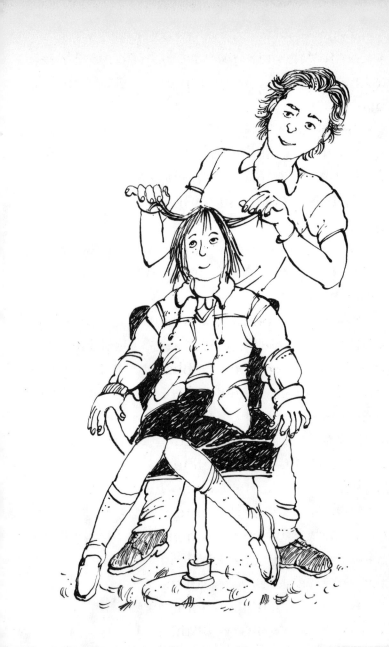

There were some clusters of grey hair under chair number two. That would be a wee old gran, just like her own, who lived down south in Newcastle. Perhaps this gran was going out to play bingo tonight, and had had her hair done specially. Then there were long soft golden curls lying beside chair number five, and there was a cushion on the chair! That was a good clue. It was sure to have been a little girl. It would have been her very first haircut, thought Siobhan. She would have been a bit nervous, but Mr Russell would have been kind, and would have made Melissa laugh by making funny faces to her in the mirror. Siobhan decided that a child with long honey-coloured locks, like a princess in a fairy-tale, would surely have a name such as Melissa.

Her mum had finished in the utility room and was now following Siobhan, mopping furiously.

'Nearly finished.' She squeezed the mop out thoroughly. 'Just the mirrors to shine up and the dusting. I think we'll treat ourselves tonight and visit the chippy on the way home.'

Siobhan wandered towards the front of the

shop, and sat down at reception. Her mum preferred to do the polishing herself. She prided herself on not leaving any smears or streaky marks. Siobhan tidied up the magazines and comics. She looked at Mr Russell's wigs, arranged in the window. He had spotlights which switched on at night to make passers-by stop and look in.

Outside it was starting to get dark. The street lights shone in the dusk. This was the season Siobhan liked the best, trees and hedges changing colour and the smell of bonfire smoke. Hallowe'en was coming soon. There would soon be bags and bags of different types of nuts and scary masks for sale.

Siobhan liked going to the chip shop. It smelled friendly and warm. She and her mum would hurry home with their steaming bags before they got cold, and have supper and watch TV together. Then she could give her mum the letter and maybe tell her about what was happening at school. She heaved a sigh. Perhaps everything would be all right now.

It was just as well Siobhan could not see into the future. Far from everything coming all right

– a catastrophe was just about to strike her!

Siobhan was so busy thinking of eating her chips later, and studying Mr Russell's window display, that she was never sure exactly what happened next.

She heard her mum call out for her to pick up the envelope while she switched off the lights in the back shop.

Siobhan got up, pulling on her anorak as she did so. She leaned on the counter and as her fingers grasped the envelope Mr Russell's new wig stand wobbled horribly.

Siobhan made a panicky grab for it. Too late! Her fingers barely brushed against it. Then it crashed on to the floor.

'YOU CLUMSY FOOL!'

Siobhan's mother was white-faced with rage. She lifted her hand to strike, and as Siobhan cowered in fear, her mother let her hand fall.

The reception area was tiled and Mr Russell's new wig stand had smashed into half a dozen pieces. Siobhan looked down. The wig stand lay at her feet. Broken and in bits. And it was her fault. Siobhan moaned and covered her face with her hands.

'Oh! Oh! I don't know what to do,' said her mum. She rushed to get the brush and shovel. 'How much do these things cost? I don't know.'

She gabbled on to herself nervously as she tidied up. 'One week's wages anyway. Maybe two or three, and the electric due. Oh! Oh!'

She turned on Siobhan harshly. 'Stop making that silly noise,' she ordered, 'and make yourself useful. Here.' She thrust the brush and shovel at her. 'Put these away. I'll write Mr Russell a note asking him to let me know the cost.' She scribbled on the outside of the envelope with her wages in it. 'I'd better leave this money as part payment.' She chewed her fingers nervously. 'All that work for nothing.'

They locked up the shop, and started up the road. Siobhan trailed behind as her mother went on and on.

And on and on. Siobhan had always found in circumstances like this that it was best not to interrupt. Even on the occasion when one had a perfectly good excuse (although this was not one of them), it was pointless to try to explain. It was as though adults needed to get all their anger talked out, and it was best just to let them get on with it. So Siobhan trudged silently behind, staring at her mother's back as her mum got it all out of her system.

'Trying to snatch a few pennies here and there. What's the point?'

Her mum had reduced her volume to an angry mutter by the time they reached their front door. She stepped aside to let Siobhan through. Siobhan had her eyes cast down as she sidled through the door, trying to make herself as inconspicuous as possible. Her mum stopped in mid-sentence as she caught sight of her face.

Siobhan went straight to her room and got ready for bed. Tomorrow was an early start. Her mum cleaned the dentist's surgery two days a week. Miss Fullerton, the dentist, liked Mrs Cunningham to come in before her patients arrived. So Siobhan and her mum left the house quite early in the morning those days. Siobhan didn't mind. Miss Fullerton always bought all the new comics as she had lots of young patients, and Siobhan got a chance to read them. It also meant she got to school earlier and so avoided the trouble-makers.

Siobhan put on her pyjamas. Her arms were stretching out of the ends of the sleeves. She must have grown some more. At this rate she would be a giantess! More expense for her mum. She pulled down her window blind. The hills were now more like those in the far north of Scotland, large and menacing, their shape now like a dark humpbacked troll watching her.

There was a soft knock on her bedroom door, and her mum came in with a tray.

'I made you some tea and toast,' she said. She put the tray down. 'I didn't mean to go on and on,' she said awkwardly. She stroked Siobhan's hair. 'I got such a fright, and I was hoping to put something aside to go and visit Gran.' She sighed. 'Not to worry.' She patted Siobhan on the head and went out.

Now Siobhan felt even worse. There was a

big lump in her throat. She gazed at the butter
congealing coldly on her toast. She couldn't eat
it at all. She got into bed and curled up small
and unhappy under her duvet.

6

Siobhan had forgotten all about the Headteacher's letter to her mum. It wasn't until she was in the school library at lunch-time the next day and she had taken her book out of her rucksack that she saw it sticking out between the pages. Her stomach did one of its horrible heaves as she picked up the brown envelope from where it had fallen on to the floor.

She shoved it quickly back into her bag as she heard footsteps coming along the corridor. It was Mrs Allan, the librarian, and she was with one of the supply teachers. The door was open a little way and Siobhan could hear their conversation.

'You've got that big girl that's in Miss Wainwright's class in there again today,' said the teacher. 'I don't know how you can stand her mooning about you all the time.'

'I like her,' said Mrs Allan stiffly, 'and she is very helpful.'

'Why doesn't she go out and play with the rest of the children? I've noticed that she doesn't seem to mix well at all.'

'And *I've* noticed that some of those children are not as nice as they appear to be,' replied Mrs Allan smartly. 'Some of them are very good at calling names.'

'Oh, there's always a bit of rough and tumble in the playground. That's a normal part of growing up,' said the teacher. 'If you ask me, a girl like that brings it on herself.'

'Actually, I did NOT ask you,' said Mrs Allan coldly. 'And I happen to believe that *nobody* brings that on themselves.'

She pushed the door of the library open and saw Siobhan standing just inside. 'Oh,' she said. She glanced back out into the corridor and shut the door firmly.

Siobhan turned and looked out of the window. It was a warm sunny day. Children were standing talking and laughing, or play-ing with ropes or balls, or running and shouting. It seemed to her that everyone

36

was outside playing. Everyone except her, that is.

She knew what would happen, though, if she went into the school yard. Karen and her friends would pass the signal for her to be left out of the game and everyone would do as she told them. Or worse could happen, as it had before. They would gang up together and follow her around, jeering and chanting, as she went from one group to the other trying to join in.

'Are you all right, Siobhan?'

'What?' Siobhan turned back.

'You haven't eaten your packed lunch.' Mrs Allan pointed at the sandwich box on the table. She leaned over and touched Siobhan on the forehead. 'You are a little hot. Perhaps I should tell Miss Wainwright that you are unwell and she can contact your mum?'

'No!' cried Siobhan in a panic. That was the last thing she wanted. Her mum would be called to the school and she had not yet told her about the letter.

'No . . . please,' she said.

'OK. OK.' said Mrs Allan. 'Stay calm.'

She studied Siobhan for a moment or two, tapping her teeth with a pencil. 'I have a suggestion. I am due to visit the Educational Resource Centre this afternoon to collect books and materials for your class project. You are doing "Our Celtic Heritage" this term. Would you like to accompany me?'

Siobhan nodded without speaking.

'Good,' said Mrs Allan. 'I'll ask Miss Wainwright for permission for you. I'll say that you are a bit under the weather and a little trip would perk you up. There is one condition, however, Siobhan.' She paused, 'You really MUST perk up.' She laughed. 'This library will come apart if its best assistant is in the doldrums all the time.'

Siobhan smiled. She did feel better. She knew she would enjoy a visit to the Resource Centre. It was a big library, with not only books but all sorts of other materials to help the schools in the area with their projects. The librarians there made up subject packs of audio-visual material, maps, books, articles and actual artefacts if possible, so that the pupils could see real examples of the culture of other lands and times.

Mrs Allan returned within a few minutes. She clapped her hands.

'Permission granted,' she said. 'Let us set off on our expedition, Siobhan, to gather information on the Celts.'

It was to be an expedition that Siobhan would never forget.

7

The Resource Centre was housed in an old building in the centre of the nearby town. The shelves were packed with books, journals, and project folders. Mrs Allan was soon organizing her collection with the help of the Resource Centre's librarian.

Siobhan glanced through some of the material. The Celts had been her forebears; there were many Celtic place names in Scotland. They had left traces of their presence all over: in burial mounds, in the High Crosses in Iona, in a silver hoard of treasure found at St Ninian's Isle off the coast of Shetland.

Siobhan and Mrs Allan took some examples of pages from illuminated manuscripts, the writing done before the printing press was invented. The scribes had decorated their scripts with bright drawings of butterflies, birds and insects. Siobhan helped roll up a magnificent wall chart which showed where the Celts had lived: from Ireland in the west to Austria in the east, and from Scotland in the north, south to Spain and northern Italy. All around the margins were colourful illustrations of the Celtic heroes, their chariots, clothes and jewellery.

The librarian had set aside all the books she thought were suitable. Siobhan packed them carefully in the 'coffins', the long wooden boxes with carry handles at each end in which the books were transported. There were books on Celtic history, on excavation of burial places, books on artwork with beautiful coloured plates inside, and some collections of folk and fairy-tales. These would be fun to read, thought Siobhan, exciting and mysterious stories of battles and treachery and romance.

'We shall go into the store now,' said Mrs Allan, 'and see what interesting things we can find.'

It was cool and quiet in the store-room. The lights were dim. The librarian explained that certain objects had to be kept away from the sun and too much heat or they would spoil.

Siobhan found it very pleasant to wander among the shelves, stopping now and then to examine something of interest. She paused where a birch-bark canoe slumbered alone on a long shelf. It had been lent to her school when they had been studying the North American Indians. She ran her fingers very gently along the surface. Real people – Red Indians – had paddled this seemingly fragile craft among swift-flowing rapids.

'Over here, Siobhan,' called Mrs Allan.

Siobhan went to the end of the stack. She turned towards the sound of Mrs Allan's voice,

and walked to the shelves signed THE CELTS.

As she reached the beginning of the row, something glittered briefly – as if the reflection of the sun had trapped its beauty. But of course there was no bright light, thought Siobhan, here in the store-room.

She looked quickly at what had attracted her eye. On the first shelf, dusty and still, lay a coiled snake. Its black jewelled eye, unlidded, unblinking, held hers. She stretched her hand out, slowly – compelled to touch this unsleeping serpent.

It moved. Faster than a gleam of lightning. A sharp stab in her hand. Did she imagine the hiss? She did not imagine the spot of bright blood which burst forth on her finger.

'Aahh,' she gasped.

'What is it?'

Mrs Allan was at her side.

'Have you found something for us to bring back?' she asked.

Siobhan sucked her finger, and nodded at the shelf.

'Mmmm,' said Mrs Allan, 'this brooch? I don't know if it is so very interesting. There are better examples of Celtic knotwork than that.'

Siobhan peered over Mrs Allan's shoulder. So it was just a brooch. It had looked so real to her, real and alive. She must have caught her finger on the pin as she touched it. Yet she had been sure . . .

Mrs Allan picked it up and turned it over in her hand.

'Celtic knotwork,' she said. 'The Celts used designs like this a great deal, regular patterns of swirls and circles and spirals.'

She turned the brooch over. 'This would have been used to hold a cloak or plaid around the wearer. Both men and women wore them. This one has a strange construction,' she said, 'something different about it. But there are other more colourful ones.'

'No, that one,' said Siobhan urgently, 'we *must* take that one.'

'Why?' laughed Mrs Allan. 'There is a rather nice copy of the Tara brooch, with all its different stones.'

'It's important that we have that one,' said Siobhan. Then she paused. Why had she said that? 'I don't know why,' she went on. 'I just have a feeling about it . . .'

'All right,' said Mrs Allan easily. She lifted up the brooch and popped it in her box. 'Now, what else?' she said, looking around.

Siobhan had the weirdest sensation as she followed Mrs Allan between the shelves. She felt that she had been here before, but that was not the case. It was as if . . . as if this was supposed to happen, as if events were taking place almost as though they had been pre-planned.

Siobhan stopped as another thought suddenly occurred to her. She felt no pain where she had jabbed her finger on the brooch. She withdrew her finger from her mouth and examined it.

There was nothing there. No mark or scratch of any kind on her skin.

8

'Keltoi were what the Greeks called them, meaning "strangers", the "people who are different" – hence the name Celts,' Mrs Allan explained, as she backed her car out of the car park and they headed towards the school. 'And it is from Greek and Roman writers that we get our information about them, because they left no written records. They passed their legends on by storytelling: the Scottish and European folk tales, tales of Merlin and King Arthur, Gawain of Wales and the princes of Ireland. It was much later that they were all written down. I'll let you have one of these books to take home with you tonight, Siobhan, and you can read all about them.'

They unpacked the car when they got back to school. Some of the material would go to Miss Wainwright's classroom, and some would stay in the library. Mrs Allan kept a separate bookcase for project books and she set out the books on this.

There was a large display case for the various items they had brought. Siobhan unpacked them carefully from their tissue paper. She rearranged the cardboard blocks inside the case and selected a deep purple satin from Mrs Allan's collection of background materials. She laid the artefacts carefully on these. A cooking pot, a highly polished bronze mirror with etched engravings, neckbands and armbands called torcs, made of twisted metal, finger rings and hair clips, glass and amber beads. At the bottom of the box lay the curled snake.

Siobhan lifted it gently from its bed. She was not the least afraid of it. Rather the opposite. She knew that it was special. Others, Mrs Allan and the staff at the Centre, had not felt the power coming from it. She knew about its power and it was a secret that only she knew. She did not know why it was special – yet.

She placed it at the very front of the case.

'There,' she said softly. 'You may see all, and all may see you.'

The snake said nothing. It did not move. It only gazed out with a quiet satisfaction from its new home.

'That's excellent,' said Mrs Allan, who had come to watch Siobhan do her finishing touches. 'Purple is just the right colour to set off these beautiful things.'

She locked up the case. 'You know a strange thing about that brooch?' she said. 'We have no information on it. It had no number in the Resource collection, and the librarians could find no trace of it being added to their stock.' She laughed. 'Another mysterious Celtic legend.'

Siobhan smiled as she closed the case. Mrs Allan's words had not surprised her at all.

'I don't particularly like it,' Mrs Allan went on. 'It's got a slightly sinister look, the way the snake's eye watches you all the time.'

'I *do* like it,' said Siobhan firmly. The intricate interwoven pattern fascinated her, the coils that seemed separate and then as you followed them around were actually part of the same.

They had worked all afternoon, and it was a good few minutes after the home-time bell had rung before Siobhan went to the cloakroom to collect her anorak.

Karen and Rosie were leaning up against the pegs close to her jacket. Siobhan's heart skipped. Why were they still here?

As she lifted her jacket they both sniggered loudly. All the cords of her anorak had been tied together. The ones for the hood and around the neck and the bottom of the jacket were all knotted and twisted with one another. It was cloudier outside now, with rain starting to fall. Siobhan could walk home carrying her jacket and get wet, no doubt with Karen and Rosie behind her laughing, or stay and undo these knots.

Siobhan gazed at her jacket. It would take hours.

Or would it?

She studied the cords carefully. It was a bit like Celtic knotwork, she thought. Twisted and complicated, yet part of the same. She fiddled with the knots gently, and then thought of the snake, coiled, yet able to straighten in a second. Her fingers moved skilfully, and the knots unravelled.

Karen and Rosie were still laughing. It sounded harsh and horrible, like a bird cawing. Well, thought Siobhan, snakes were faster than birds, silent and deadly. She swung her jacket on around her shoulders and they stopped at once. With one triumphant glance at them Siobhan marched out of the school.

9

Siobhan's elation only lasted until she got
home. As she turned the corner at the end of
her street she saw Mr Russell, the hairdresser,
coming out of her block of flats. She stopped
and pretended to look at the nearest shop
window.

Why was he visiting her mum? It would be
about the wig stand. Siobhan kicked a stone
into the gutter as she slouched along towards
her home. If he had actually come to the house
then it must be serious. Perhaps he had told her
mum not to come back.

She let herself into the flat very quietly. She
could hear her mum in the kitchen. The radio
was on and there was the sound of the table
being set for tea. Siobhan crept softly down the
hall to her own room.

She sat down at her desk and looked at

herself in the mirror above it. Up until this term at school she had never thought about how she looked. It didn't seem to matter. Now it did. It had suddenly become important to be roughly the same as everyone else. And she wasn't.

Her hair was black, too black, and it hung so straight down each side of her head that it was boring. *And* she was too big, she took up too much room. Beside everyone else in the class she was the Jolly Giant. Except that she wasn't jolly. Siobhan sighed. She had been jolly once. It seemed a long time ago. Rosie had been her friend, then Karen had taken her away from her.

Siobhan looked at her hands. They were huge. She knew this for a fact. When they had been studying volume and space at school, Miss Wainwright had got everyone to draw around their hands and Siobhan's had been the biggest – by a mile. They were even bigger than Miss Wainwright's.

She was like the Celts, she thought, the 'Keltoi', the ones who were different.

Siobhan stretched her hands out in front of her. She covered her face with them and then

peered at herself in the mirror. She caught sight of her little bank box sitting beside the mirror. She had been saving to go to Gran's. She opened it up and counted the money. Four pounds and thirty-eight pence. It wasn't an awful lot.

She scooped it up and went down the hall to the kitchen.

'There you are,' said her mum, 'I didn't hear you come in.'

Siobhan put the money on the table.

'That's to go towards the wig stand. I'm really sorry, Mum. I don't know what happened. It just seemed to fall over.' She looked down at her hands. 'I'm so big, big and clumsy.'

'Don't talk that way about yourself.' Her mum came over and put her hands around Siobhan's shoulders. 'I shouted last night because I got a fright, and because I was angry, and I should say sorry to you.' She gave Siobhan a quick kiss on the cheek.

'And in any case it wasn't you to blame. The wig stand was faulty. Mr Russell had left it out to return it to the rep. today. The base was uneven. It probably toppled when you leaned on the counter. He came round specially a few minutes ago to tell me and give me my money. He says that you wouldn't even need to have touched it for it to fall over.'

Siobhan felt a tremendous feeling of relief sweep over her. It hadn't been her clumsiness after all.

Her mum stood back from her and studied her critically.

'You are NOT too big,' she said firmly. 'You are a teeny-weeny bit taller than the rest of your class. But it could be that they are a little short for their years. They'll soon catch you up. People grow at different rates. *And* you are not clumsy. Every time I meet Miss Wainwright and Mrs Allan they witter on about how helpful you are. It's embarrassing sometimes.'

Later on, in bed with her pillows all propped up at her back Siobhan opened the book Mrs Allan had given her to read at home. It was about the Ancient Tales of an Ancient People, a collection of different legends and fairy stories from Celtic lands. She ran her eye down the list on the contents page. They were all stirring titles:

'The Wild Geese.'

'Cormac's Cup of Gold.'

'Neil of the Nine Hostages.'

'The Countess of the Fountain.'

'Tristan and Iseult.'

And then, last of all:

'Siobhan of the Seven Valleys.'

Her own name! That would be the story which she would read first, Siobhan decided.

She turned to the last legend in the book.

10

Siobhan started to read the story . . .

In the land where the last rays of the setting sun meet the first rays of the rising dawn, there dwelt a beautiful Princess.

She was tall as the reeds that grow by the lakeside, and her hair was long and black and flowed down from her forehead like falling rain. The land in which she lived contained Seven Valleys, one for every day of the week and each more lovely than the other. Her father, the King, had died, leaving his sorrowing daughter mourning and weeping.

'Guard my kingdom and protect my people well,' he had instructed her on his deathbed. 'There are enemies to the East and to the West, and to the North and to the South. They are greedy and cruel, and they will tell lies about you and try to use you ill. They will come singly and in groups of many, and try to take what you have.'

He laid his hand heavily on his daughter's head. 'When I leave you, you will own these Seven Valleys, these people will be yours, and you will be their Princess.'

'How can I do this, Father?' cried his daughter, 'when I am only a child?'

The King wore a long cloak made of silver and gold with much richly coloured embroidered work upon it. It was fastened across the shoulder by one single plaid pin. This brooch took the form of many swirls and twists but was in fact a single snake coiled in upon itself. A snake made of beaten silver with one glittering black stone as an eye.

'Take this,' said her father, unfastening the brooch and handing it to her. 'This is my Plaid Pin. The serpent who never sleeps will guard you and guide you, and give you strength to vanquish all your enemies. Use its power wisely and well.'

Then the King closed his eyes for the last time. His daughter bent her head and wept bitterly.

Not long after her father's funeral her enemies came as he had foretold. They plotted and schemed against her, and came to her court and spoke their wicked lies. And Siobhan held the Plaid Pin in her hand and she felt its power, the power that was hers, and she was more skilful and swift than they were, and her tongue was more clever and cunning. And she defeated them in words and wisdom.

Whereupon they raised mighty armies against her, with many spears and warriors. And Siobhan led her people into battle in her chariot. With the Plaid Pin on her shoulder she was victorious. The eye of the serpent destroyed all that it saw, and Siobhan swept them aside. From the North and the South she defeated them, and from the East.

At last one day came a messenger from the lands in the West. This messenger came alone, and he was tall and fair and handsome, and around his head he wore a circlet of gold studded with rubies.

'I am the Prince of the West,' he said, 'and I do not come to make war with you, Siobhan of the Seven Valleys.'

And Siobhan saw into his heart and knew this to be true. And as they looked at each other they fell in love. And they were married and lived together many long years in happiness with many adventures as well.

And on their wedding day the people of the Seven Valleys made a carpet of flowers for them to walk upon. And as her servants braided her hair for her marriage ceremony, Siobhan of the Seven Valleys looked at the Plaid Pin and knew that she had no longer need of it. She had used its power

wisely. Her battles had been fought and won.

So, as she walked forward on her wedding morning to embrace her Prince, she cast the serpent from her and it fell down among the flowers at her feet. And to this day no one knows its whereabouts.

Some say it rolled down and down into the earth to the land of Tir-na-n'Og.

Some say the fairies stole it.

Some say the snake became a living one and slithered away.

The legend says that Siobhan will have need of it again one day. When her enemies surround her, with their snares and swords, their evil deeds and wicked ways, then the snake will seek her out. She will not have to search for the Plaid Pin. It will come to her.

Siobhan will hold the Plaid Pin once more in her hand and its power will be hers. And when she has it in her keeping, and her enemies come, then let them come. She will conquer all.

Siobhan closed the book and stared straight ahead.

Tomorrow morning at school, Siobhan decided, I will go straight to the display case in the library and check the pattern on the brooch.

She would bring the book of legends with her and see if the design illustrated in it matched.

But I don't have to, she thought.

She *knew* that in the serpent nestling on its bed of purple silk lay the lost Plaid Pin of Siobhan of the Seven Valleys.

11

It was the same!

Siobhan's hand shook as she held the book beside the brooch. She had rushed to school as early as possible the next day, taken the key from where Mrs Allan kept it and unlocked the case. She laid the brooch on the page beside the illustration coloured in reds and blues and greens. It showed Siobhan of the Seven Valleys in her chariot, her long black hair flowing out behind her. The design of the brooch was clear in every detail. The two matched exactly.

What she, Siobhan Cunningham, had in her hand was the Plaid Pin.

Her fingers closed around it. It glowed warm in her palm.

'Hello, Siobhan. You are in early today.'

Siobhan jumped. She had not heard Mrs Allan come into the library.

'Are you looking at the brooch again? It seems to fascinate you.'

'Mrs Allan, may I ask a favour?' said Siobhan. 'Would you let me wear the Plaid – the brooch, just for a little while?'

Mrs Allan hesitated.

'Please?' said Siobhan. 'I will be extra specially careful.'

'I suppose it can't do any harm,' said Mrs Allan slowly. 'Though please do not go out of the school with it. Here, I will pin it on for you, and please don't take it off all day.'

Siobhan gave Mrs Allan the Plaid Pin. She looked down at her own hand. Clearly embedded on her palm was the outline of the snake.

She smiled. She had the power.

The first person she met as she walked towards the cloakroom was Rosie. Siobhan looked at her scornfully.

'How long did it take you to tie my anorak cords in knots yesterday, Rosie?' she asked.

Rosie didn' t say anything, but her face went a bit pink.

Siobhan marched past her along the corridor.

'Rosie-red-face,' she said loudly.

Harry Morgan, who was hanging up his jacket, turned his head in amazement.

'Did you notice how warm it's become all of a sudden?' Siobhan asked him innocently. 'It must be the heat from Rosie's red face.'

Benny had arrived in the cloakroom.

'You leave her alone,' he said.

Siobhan touched the Plaid Pin. She traced the form of the snake under her finger. Then she drew herself up to her full height. She was much taller than Benny.

'Do not threaten me,' she declared, as Siobhan of the Seven Valleys had done to her enemy from the North. She stepped forward, and Benny stepped backwards and hurried away.

At break-time it was wet outside and most of the class stayed in the cloakroom. Harry went home at lunch-time, but at morning break he and Siobhan usually sat together. He would tell her all about his pets. He had two rabbits, a guinea-pig and a hamster. Harry took great care of them. Siobhan had gone over to his home once or twice during the summer holidays and helped him clean out their hutches.

This morning Siobhan decided to do something different. She sat up on the window-sill swinging her legs and looking down on the other children talking and moving around below her. She could see Karen and her little group in one corner whispering. They kept glancing in her direction. Let them, she thought.

The bell rang and she jumped down and made her way back to the classroom. Karen stepped in front of her.

'I want to see you,' she said.

Siobhan's lip curled.

'I do not have the time just now,' she said. 'I will deal with you later.' And she swept regally past Karen into the classroom.

Lunch-time came and Siobhan decided to eat her packed lunch in the cloakroom. She noticed that Karen did not have so many people around her as she ate her sandwiches. Siobhan chewed slowly. Every time Karen looked over Siobhan would stare hard back at her and then Karen would look away first.

Siobhan smiled to herself. She had the power.

At home-time Siobhan saw Karen standing

just inside the front door. A group of classmates hung around a bit further back. Karen had taken Harry's schoolbag and was swinging it high above her head.

'Jump, little doggie,' Karen teased him, holding it up just out of his reach. Harry tried desperately to grab his schoolbag. Karen pulled it away. 'Beg for your bag, like a good little pup,' she said.

'Stop that!' cried Siobhan angrily.

Karen turned to see who was speaking to her.

'Make me!' she said menacingly.

Siobhan clasped the Plaid Pin firmly in her hand. The black jewelled eye of the snake pricked her finger sharply.

'Now,' she vowed, as Siobhan of the Seven Valleys had done to her enemy from the East. 'Tyrant, your time has come!'

And stepping forward, Siobhan smacked Karen hard across her face.

That night Siobhan gave her mother the Head-teacher's letter.

'Why didn't you show me this earlier?' her mum asked her.

Siobhan shrugged.

'I was upset about the wig stand.'

'I knew you were out of sorts about something. I just thought that you had a virus,' said her mum. 'I wish you had told me before, Siobhan.'

Siobhan looked away. She hadn't had the courage before.

'I will come tomorrow afternoon and speak to the Head,' said her mum.

The next day, first thing, Siobhan went to the library.

'I have great need of you,' she whispered, as she lifted the snake from its bed of purple satin. Its black eye gazed at her steadily.

When Mrs Allan came into the library Siobhan asked her if she could wear the brooch again. The librarian frowned and looked at her.

'Siobhan, you and I have always been friends,' she said, 'so I must be honest with you. There is something about your fascination with that thing which makes me uneasy.' She laughed. 'You are almost a different girl when you have it in your possession.'

I am, thought Siobhan silently. I am the other Siobhan. I own the power.

'Really?' she said aloud to Mrs Allan. 'I won't ask again. It's just that I found a story about a brooch in that book you gave me.' She pointed to the book which she had returned. 'The heroine's name was the same as mine. I was playing at being a princess.'

'Oh, very well,' said Mrs Allan, 'one more time.'

Siobhan closed her eyes as Mrs Allan pinned the brooch on. This afternoon would be the interview with the Head and her mum. She needed its power.

There was quite a group gathered in the cloakroom as she arrived. Karen was standing a little to one side, and so was Harry Morgan. He was chewing his lip and fiddling with his rucksack.

Siobhan sneered at Karen.

'Karen the Coward,' she said. 'Karen Cabbage. Karen Kangaroo, Karen Cow.'

Someone laughed. A few others joined in.

'Moooooooo . . .' added Siobhan nastily.

Karen picked up her schoolbag and started to leave the cloakroom. As she came level with her, Siobhan moved forward quickly and bumped into Karen very hard. Karen gasped as her back was pushed into a coat-peg. Her eyes filled with tears.

Siobhan strode into the classroom ahead of the rest. She had the power. She could destroy her enemies. Now she knew how it felt. She sat down at her desk. She was alone. She looked about her. Harry had gone to sit across the aisle.

'Why have you moved?' Siobhan asked him.

He did not meet her gaze.

'Why?' she asked again.

'I didn't think you were like that, Siobhan,' he said.

'Like what?' She was totally bewildered.

'A name-caller,' he said miserably.

'You mean because I called names at Karen?' said Siobhan.

'And the rest,' said Harry. 'You've changed, Siobhan, you're different. The way you walk and talk and look. You're starting to become like them.'

'Just because I stand up for myself?' Siobhan demanded.

'You're doing more than just standing up for yourself,' said Harry miserably. 'Siobhan, you hit Karen. You slapped her right across her face, and you hurt her in the cloakroom.'

'Somebody like that deserves it.'

Siobhan suddenly stopped speaking. She had heard that phrase before. And recently. Then she remembered. In the corridor outside the library – the conversation she had overheard. About herself. And what had Mrs Allan said? *Nobody* deserves to be treated like that. She looked across the room at Karen. Her head was down on her desk. The way she, Siobhan, used to sit.

Now she was as Karen had been. Harry said nothing more. He only looked away from her.

Then Siobhan remembered the story of the Plaid Pin. How in the end, when Siobhan of the Seven Valleys no longer needed the power of the Pin to defeat her enemies, she had let it go.

At lunch-time Siobhan walked firmly in the direction of the library. She knew what she had to do. Mrs Allan was sitting at her desk reading. Siobhan unfastened the Plaid Pin and placed it on the desk.

'I've decided not to wear it any more,' she said.

Mrs Allan looked up and smiled at her.

'A wise decision, I think,' she said. She showed Siobhan the book she was reading. It was the book of Celtic legends. 'I was reading about your namesake,' she said. 'The tall and beautiful Siobhan, with the black hair.' She smiled gently at Siobhan. 'And with the help of the unsleeping snake she destroyed her enemies.' She waited a moment. 'But you do not want to destroy anyone, do you, Siobhan?'

Siobhan shook her head.

'What do you do if you are being picked on?' she asked. 'You can only say nothing or fight back.'

Mrs Allan shook her head.

'There is a third choice,' she said. 'And it is the hardest of all to make. You can tell someone about it.'

'My mum is coming in later,' said Siobhan, 'to see the Head.'

'Well then,' said Mrs Allan, 'tell them both exactly what is happening.'

Siobhan fingered the brooch which lay between them on the desk.

'It gives me the power,' she said, 'as it gave it to Siobhan of the Seven Valleys.'

'But Siobhan of the Seven Valleys knew to let it go,' said Mrs Allan. 'She used it to protect her people and then she cast it aside.'

'I suppose that the strength will stay with me,' said Siobhan slowly, 'that I will be strong enough to speak out. But if I continue to use the snake then I will be tempted to go further.'

'Yes,' said Mrs Allan. 'The strength is in the USE of power. If you go further then you ABUSE it.'

Siobhan was called to the Head's study in the early afternoon. As she passed the open door to the school yard she looked outside. It was turning into a fine autumn afternoon. A day to be outside playing, before the cold winter arrived, which it did early in this part of Scotland. She would ask her mum if Harry could come with them when they started berrying.

Her mum was sitting with the Head when she arrived and they had obviously been discussing her.

'Sit down, Siobhan,' said the Headteacher. 'I've just been talking to your mother. It would appear that you had a little upset at home which may have affected your behaviour?'

Siobhan said nothing.

'Of course,' the Head went on, 'you had been having problems in school before that.' She paused for a moment. 'Mrs Allan, the librarian, had a brief word with me.'

Siobhan looked up at this. The Head smiled at her.

'School life is full of problems,' she said kindly, 'ups and downs of all sorts. Please try in future to talk to someone, anyone at all, when you reach one of the downs.' She waited. 'Mrs Allan said that you might have something to say to me.'

Siobhan thought of Siobhan of the Seven Valleys. She would have spoken up in the high clear voice of a princess to defend her good name.

'I was being picked on,' she said. 'They do it all the time to different people. This time it was my turn. I just couldn't talk to anyone about it.'

Siobhan's mum put her arm around her.

'You can always talk to me,' she said.

'Now,' said the Head, 'I understand that the problem may have resolved itself. However, I am going to have a brief word with Karen Williams. Just a general chat, although I'm sure that she will know what I'm getting at. And if you have any worries in the future, please, please tell me.'

As they left the office Siobhan's mother stopped to speak to the school secretary. Siobhan went into the corridor and walked straight into Karen Williams.

'I'm going to get you,' said Karen.

'No, you are not,' said Siobhan firmly, but not nastily. 'I do not fear you any more. Your power is broken for ever.' She had without knowing it used the words of Siobhan of the Seven Valleys when she dealt with her last enemy from the South.

Weeks later Siobhan helped Mrs Allan return the books and project materials to the Resource Centre. She had enjoyed learning about the Celts, their warrior ways, their gods, their language and their distinctive style of art. She could see their influence in some of the present-day art of modern Scotland, an influence from many hundreds of years ago. It was part of her own culture. Their stories and history were also hers.

They unpacked the boxes and ticked every-

thing off the checklist. Then they returned the items to the store.

Siobhan laid the Plaid Pin carefully back in its place on the shelf. In the half light the black eye of the snake winked at her.

It would always be there for her, thought Siobhan, as she walked away, or perhaps for some other who had need of it. She closed the door.

In the dark, on the shelf, the coiled snake rested its head and waited.

END

IT HAPPENS

It happens in the playground
It happens in the loo
They wait outside the school gate
Just to pick on you

Torment you, taunt you, call you names
Won't let you join in any games

It happens at the bus stop
It happens in the class

They always know the right time
No adult walking past

Push you, pull you, nip and squeeze
Saying cruel things, just to tease

It happens in the corridor
It happens in the yard
They used to be your pals once
Now they hit you – hard

Take your sweets and crisps and money
Laugh at you, pretend it's funny

It happens all the time
No-one's ever there to see
What I'd like to know is,
Why's it always me?

© Theresa Breslin

WHAT IS BULLYING?

Name-calling and making cruel remarks.

Teasing and taunting.

Leaving someone out.

Pushing and shoving.

Demanding sweets, crisps or money.

Threatening behaviour.

Shouting and swearing at someone.

Damaging other people's belongings.

Fighting, hitting, punching, kicking.

Do you do this?

OR . . .

Does it happen to you?

It happened to Siobhan in this story, *Bullies at School*. She was lonely and unhappy. She didn't want to go to school. She felt sick. She had no-one to play with, no-one to talk to.
Then Siobhan found the snake brooch which seemed to help her. Wearing the Plaid Pin gave Siobhan the courage to face up to her tormen-tors. But in the end Siobhan managed without the brooch. She took it off and spoke out. She told an adult what was happening. She told the bully to leave her alone.

Perhaps you could show this book to a teacher in your school and your class could talk about Siobhan and the bullies.

Did you know that:
Bullies are cowards.
They usually pick on a person who is weaker than they are.

They gang up, two or three or more against one.

Did you know that:
You don't have to be brave to be a bully.
But you *do* have to be brave to be BULLY-PROOF.
What can you do if you, or someone you know, is being bullied?

HOW TO BE BULLYPROOF

DON'T

DON'T join in with teasing and taunting others.

DON'T buy bullies off with sweets or money.

DON'T hit back.

DO

DO TELL SOMEONE. It doesn't make you a sneak/grass/tell-tale.

DO try to stay with larger groups of people.

DO shout 'NO!' or 'GO AWAY!' in a loud voice.

DO try to stay away from places where bullies hang around.

DO remember

IT IS NOT YOUR FAULT.

USEFUL CONTACTS

CHILD LINE   TEL (FREE) 0800 1111
                       FREEPOST 1111
                       London N1 0BR

KIDSCAPE   152 Buckingham
                       Palace Road
                       London
                       SW1W 9TR
                       071 730 3300

ABC (Anti-   18 Elmgate Gardens
bullying Campaign)   Edgware
                       Middlesex HA8 9RT
                       071 378 1446/7/8/9

Campaign Against   72 Lakelands Ave.
Bullying   Upper Kilmacud Rd.
(Ireland)   Stillorgan
                       Co. Dublin

Bullying booklist   Albany Book Company
                       30 Clydeholm Road
                       Glasgow G14 0BJ

Scottish Schools   Scottish Council for
Anti-Bullying   Research in Education
Initiative   15 St John Street
                       Edinburgh EH8 8JR

Also by Theresa Breslin and available as a
Canongate Kelpie

Bullies at School
Different Directions
Simon's Challenge

If you enjoyed this Kelpie and would like a
free Kelpie sticker and catalogue
please contact:

Customer Services
Canongate Books Ltd
14 High Street
Edinburgh EH1 1TE
or email canon.gate@almac.co.uk